Stand By Me

Ruth Barringham

Also by Ruth Barringham

Playing For Real

Two Weeks In Corfu

Chapter 1

Lola was laid on the bed with Daniel. She raised one leg in the air.

'I've always had great legs.'

Beside her, Daniel looked at her raised leg and ran his hand along her thigh.

'I've always loved your legs.'

'What about the rest of me?'

He dropped his hand and turned his head to look at her. 'Feeling insecure are we?'

She lowered her leg and looked him straight in the eye. 'Well it's hard not to when I have to share you with another woman.'

Daniel looked up at the ceiling and let out a heavy sigh. 'Please let's not get into *this* again. I've told you before. I haven't had sex with my wife for years.'

'But you still live with her so she sees you a lot more than I do.'

'Lola...don't.'

Now it was her turn to sigh deeply. 'I know you don't like it when I bring it up and I know you've tried to explain it to me before, but I just don't get it. I want to. But I don't.

'Here we are laying naked in bed together in the middle of the afternoon. You could stay and have dinner with me followed by a bottle of wine and more great sex. But instead you want to go home to your wife, who you say you don't love, yet you'd rather stand by her than stand by me.'

Daniel was silent for a few moments. Then he sat up, swung his legs off the bed and reached down to the floor for his clothes.

'I can't do this anymore. When I married my wife I made a commitment. How I feel about her isn't her fault. She's not a bad person. She needs me and I won't leave her.'

'I need you too, but you keep leaving me.' Lola knew she sounded sulky, but she couldn't help it.

Daniel, now fully dressed, turned to look at her. 'If I was the type of guy who would walk out on someone who needed me just because I'd changed my mind about how I felt, then I wouldn't be the man you fell in love with. This is me, Lola. It's who I am. I never promised you more than we have and I'm tired of arguing over this.'

He turned and left the room. Within a few seconds she heard the click of the front door as it closed behind him.

Lola laid there for a few minutes going over it in her mind without having any direct thoughts.

With her mind still preoccupied with her relationship with Daniel, she went to the bathroom to shower, put on her nightshirt and dressing gown, tidied the bed, went into the living room, put on the TV and prepared herself an early dinner.

She thought about how she'd met Daniel two years ago when he'd come into her shop.

Lola owned a new age shop in the city. She'd bought it with the money from her divorce from David.

They'd been married for seven years, during which time they'd both had full-time jobs.

David loved fine living, eating out, their large house and living in luxury.

He was a lawyer when she met him and during their marriage he'd sat his Bar Exams and became a barrister.

He helped prosecute criminals and he was good at it too. But his job entailed working long hours and he'd often work at home at the weekends too.

Lola had worked in retail as a department manager at a large store. She'd loved her work although David sometimes sneered at her low income compared to his large salary.

But money had never been a priority for Lola. She preferred to have more free time and while David pursued his career, she looked after their home including making all her own curtains, blinds and bedspreads and turning their garden into a food paradise with fruit trees and vegetable beds that flourished.

Living in a Brisbane suburb in Australia wasn't ideal growing conditions and most people struggled to grow anything in the dry, humid climate. But Lola was a keen gardener and a nature person, so she enjoyed spending time outdoors putting her hands to the soil.

But their diverse personalities meant that eventually she and David had nothing in common.

After seven years of marriage the 'itch' to leave their relationship surfaced, so they amicably parted.

And because they lived in a large, expensive house, there was enough equity in it for Lola to buy a small house in the suburbs and open a new age shop in the heart of the city.

She didn't work there full-time because she had two employees who worked full-time plus a part-time single mum who worked almost every day and brought her daughter to work with her on weekends and school holidays.

The shop also had a resident tarot card reader at the weekends, but she worked freelance and rented a small back room where she did her readings.

So Lola didn't need to work much herself because she was lucky enough to have staff who were intelligent and able to all work together and keep the place running.

She'd owned the shop for four years and was happily single and unattached when Daniel walked into her life.

He'd come in to buy scented candles. Lola thought that he didn't seem like the scented candle type so he must have been buying them for someone else.

She had served him herself, helping him pick out some candles and nice holders. When she asked if he'd like them all gift-wrapped, he said yes.

Something about him struck her when he walked into the shop that day. She knew he felt it too because as she stared at him, he stared straight back and smiled at her.

Since leaving David, Lola had decided to stay single and never got romantically involved with anyone ever again. She thought marriage wasn't all it was cracked up to be. She found it boring and could see no advantage to living with someone else, so apart from a few short dates, she stayed happily single.

But Daniel was different. As soon as she saw him, she felt an instant attraction that she couldn't explain. She could tell that he felt it too.

He was small for a man, stocky and had short blonde hair and blue eyes. Lola didn't even think he was her type but there was just something about him.

They chatted that day as she gift-wrapped his purchases. He told her that he worked as a manager in the city office of a large construction company and she told him about buying the shop.

As she handed him his gift-wrapped items, he stared at the package for a few seconds then looked her straight in the eyes and asked 'Would you like to go across the road and have coffee?' His empty hand gestured towards the café across the road.

'Hell yeah, I want to have coffee with you,' she thought, grateful that he wanted to stay longer with her. What she actually said to him was, 'Sure, why not?'

'See you soon George,' she said over her shoulder to her wide-eyed employee who had been standing beside her, as she grabbed her handbag from under the counter and headed out the door with Daniel.

Two years later and here she was, standing in the kitchen making a salad and wondering if she'd blown it and their relationship was over.

As she sliced a tomato into wedges she looked out the window. The view of the back garden was beautiful, but at the moment it didn't impress her. She was too busy wondering if she'd ever see Daniel again.

Chapter 2

Lola woke up the next morning with a feeling of apprehension, still wondering if she'd hear from Daniel.

He was the one that contacted her most of the time. They would sometimes get together by prior arrangement, but usually by surprise, depending on when he could get away from his wife.

She never called him on his mobile phone and he never called her. She didn't even have his number. That was her own choosing so that she'd never be tempted to call him at home.

She wasn't even sure where his home was. Lola lived in Windsor, which was a suburb next to the city itself on the north side. Daniel lived on the south side across the Brisbane River in a suburb called Yeronga. But she had no idea of his address and didn't want to know, otherwise she'd be too tempted to do a drive by just to be nosey and see where he lived.

It would just be her kind of luck that the day she did pass by he would be out in the front yard with his wife, glaring as she slowly cruised by staring at them both. Boy, that wouldn't look too suspicious, would it?

That's why she preferred to only have his office number, just in case, and she rarely ever called him at work.

They didn't see each other every day but they did meet up two or three times a week.

Sometimes they'd have a meal together at her place or in a restaurant in a suburb far, far away so that they wouldn't be seen by anyone who knew Daniel or his wife.

There had been numerous occasions when he'd come to her shop after work and they'd share a bottle of wine in the back room, sitting at the small staff table with only one candle for light to make it look as though the place was empty from outside.

Many times during these after-work visits they would pull their chairs closer and fondle each other's inner thighs, before moving their fingers further up and fondling each other intimately until they couldn't stand it any longer and would eagerly tear each other's clothes off. Daniel would either bend her over the table, throw her on the floor or press her up against the wall and enter her.

Lola smiled to herself and felt a tingle of excitement just thinking about those back room encounters.

There were sometimes several days when they didn't see each other at all because Daniel would have to work in the offices at a remote building site now and again, which was several hours away by plane and car. Thankfully it didn't happen too often.

And there were other times when his wife wouldn't see him for several days because he'd tell her he was working away and spend a few days with Lola instead, either at her house or they'd meet in a hotel in the country where they were unlikely to run into anyone they knew.

Those were great days. Just the two of them with nothing else to do except be together and enjoy each other.

It was during these times that Lola almost forgot that the rest of the world existed. They would spend the whole time cocooned in their own world that contained only the two of them.

They'd lose all track of time. Sleeping when they were tired, waking up together, making love over and over, eating if they were hungry and only knowing if it was day or night by how light or dark it was outside.

Yet as much as she loved Daniel and loved being with him, she was also grateful for her alone time when she got home.

She was too independent to need to be with someone else all the time. She liked to be in control of her own life and not share that control with anyone.

That's why it suited her that Daniel didn't want to live with her.

But on the other hand, it niggled at her that he was so attached to his wife.

She knew it was true that he and his wife had no sex life, because he was always hungry for her body if they hadn't seen each other for a few days and he ejaculated more quickly. That was a sure sign that he hadn't had sex because he was more needy for her than usual.

So why did he stay with his wife? And why did he feel so compelled to stand by her?

He obviously didn't love her or he wouldn't be having a relationship with someone else.

Perhaps he was right, that he really was such a caring and considerate person and honoring the vows he made to his wife at their wedding was simply a part of who he was.

A week went by and Lola didn't hear from him.

She used the extra time it gave her to catch up on a few things that needed doing at home and at work including buying in new lines of stock for the shop.

She also spent more time at work. She told herself it was because she had things to do there and wouldn't admit to herself that she was hoping to see Daniel.

She hoped every afternoon that he'd turn up at closing, sit in the back room with her, share a bottle of wine in candlelight and push her roughly against the wall.

But each day went by with no sign of him.

After two weeks, she was in a silently panic.

She tried not to show it, but George and his partner Angus, who also worked in the shop, both seemed to know.

They kept putting their arms around her waist when they spoke to her or draped their arms across her shoulders.

If they were women, they would have been asking her all kinds of questions to find out what was wrong.

Instead, they sensed her sadness and made physical gesture that said 'I feel your pain' or 'I'm here for you' without commenting.

Their small physical touches seemed a way of saying 'there, there,' like a mother comforting a child.

It was sweet. It was just what she needed.

Although she waited in hope every day that Daniel would appear, she wasn't even sure what she'd say to him even if he did.

And despite the fact that she'd goaded him about staying with his wife, she never really expected him to leave her. She wasn't looking for a full-time relationship. She just sometimes felt envious that there was another woman having a relationship with her man.

Daniel had never left her like this before. He'd never walked out.

What if he didn't come back?

What if she never saw him again?

The thought horrified her and gave her a sick, sinking feeling in the pit of her stomach.

Why had she needed to goad him again?

She no longer cared that he was married. She just wanted him back in her life again.

She wanted to cry.

A few days into the third week without Daniel, he walked into the shop at lunchtime.

Lola had just arrived and was speaking with Angus when he walked through the door.

He looked angry, or maybe it was sad. Lola wasn't sure.
'We need to talk.'
'Now?'
'Tonight. I'll come to your place at 6.30.'
'OK.'
He turned and walked away.
Lola and Angus exchanged worried looks.
'What do you think he meant?' she asked.
Angus drew in a deep breath. 'Hard to say.'
'Do you think he hasn't forgiven me?'
'Sweetheart,' said Angus without even knowing what Lola had to be forgiven for. 'If he hadn't forgiven you, he wouldn't want to see you.'
He put his arm around her shoulders. She hugged him, resting her head on his chest.
'Thanks Angus.'
His words made sense. She hoped he was right. Or was he coming round to say goodbye?
Lola would find out in about six hours.
It was going to be a long afternoon.

Chapter 3

At 6.30 exactly there was a knock at her door.

Lola felt an adrenalin rush of relief, glad to have another chance to see Daniel again and try and repair their relationship.

And she was sure that he would want her back, because as Angus said, if he hadn't forgiven her, he wouldn't have asked to see her.

'Hi,' she greeted him.

'Hi.' He looked worried. Perhaps he was uncertain of her reaction to his visit.

She stepped to one side and he walked passed her and went into the living room.

Lola closed the front door and followed him.

He turned and looked at her. 'I've missed you.'

That was all she needed to hear. She stepped forward and threw her arms around him.

They embraced tightly, their hungry mouths finding each other's.

They kissed long and hard, their tongues connecting, and entering each other's mouth.

Daniel's hands moved from her back to her sides and slid over her waist down to her hips.

She let out a soft moan. She'd missed his touch. She loved the way his hands felt on her body, the way he moved them as though he was moulding her out of clay.

She ran the palms of her hands over his chest. She loved to touch his body and knew every inch of it intimately. At the feel of her touch, he inhaled, his chest rising, and held his breathe for a moment before releasing it.

His hands moved up from her hips to her breasts.

Lola released herself from his kiss, and let out a slow breathe as her body orgasmed.

Daniel kissed her neck, mouthing different parts of her skin. She moaned loudly.

He dropped his hands, grabbed the bottom of her cotton top, lifted it up over her head and arms in one fluid motion, and put his mouth to one of her breasts.

She shivered with pleasure and could feel his erection pressing against her body.

She took a small step backwards. Daniel took a small step forwards at the same time.

They kept walking this way as Daniel unhooked her bra and removed it, his mouth seeking her nipple. She put one hand up the back of his shirt while cupping his testicles through the thin material of his pants with her other.

Their small, awkward steps eventually led them into the bedroom and to the edge of the bed where Daniel pushed her gently back onto the mattress and laid beside her, their hands never leaving each other's body the whole time.

They quickly undressed each other, wanting it to last longer but both too eager to slow down.

Once naked, she hugged him, feeling the length of his naked body against her own. The feeling was so incredible it made her orgasm again.

She lowered her head and began to kiss him all the way down his body, starting with his neck.

Daniel moaned loudly, excited with anticipation, because he knew where this was leading. They both did. And they couldn't wait.

*

When Lola awoke the next morning, she laid there for a while, basking in the memories of the night before. In her mind she relived the highlights of kissing her way down his body and all the things she had done to pleasure him. Oh God. It had been wonderful.

Sadly, he'd had to leave about an hour later, but it was long enough for them to shower, dress, and enjoy a glass of wine together, sitting out on the back patio.

Lola lived in a small wooden house that had a front verandah and a large covered, wooden patio at the back.

The house was on a large plot of land that Lola was busy landscaping and setting up vegetable beds and herbaceous borders.

The borders were looking good and she had so many trees and bushes around the perimeter near the fences, that the back yard and patio were very private.

Sitting out there last night with Daniel was heavenly. They had sat on her sofa swing and sipped wine. He sat against the arm, propped up with a cushion and she had leaned her back against him, his arm draped over her shoulder. And once again everything felt alright in her world.

Until, of course, he got up to leave, to go back to his wife.

Lola threw back the covers and got out of bed quickly. She didn't want to think about Daniel being with his wife.

But why was she so jealous about it lately?

She knew that they weren't having sex and she didn't want to live with him, so why did it bother her that he lived with someone else?

She really didn't understand her own feelings.

Unless...

What if she was wrong? What if she really did want to live with him?

No. That was stupid. Surely if she wanted to live with him she'd know it. Wouldn't she?

She pondered it as she dressed and had breakfast.

She knew that she didn't feel any urge to have him living with her yet she didn't like the fact that he lived with another woman. So what did that mean?

Was she just selfish and simply didn't want to live with him but didn't want anyone else to live with him either?

What if he lived alone? Was that what she wanted? Did she want him to be alone when he wasn't with her?

She didn't think so because she didn't care that he was with other people at work all day.

What if Daniel decided to leave his wife and come and live with her instead?

She tried to imagine what it would be like if Daniel came round with a suitcase or two full of all his worldly possessions and started unpacking them at her house.

No. That scenario didn't seem right. Not for her.

Lola had lived alone for six years, thirteen if you counted the time she was married to David because he was such a career-chasing workaholic that she hardly ever saw him and spent most of her time home alone.

But she didn't mind. She'd always been what most people would call a 'lone wolf' and had never had much need for the company of others so she had very few friends, if any at all.

She was now quite happy to be in her own company most of the time and was busy enough with her shop, her relationship with Daniel and her garden.

Speaking of which, she thought to herself, that was the ideal place to spend the rest of the day.

Everything was up-to-date at work so she wasn't needed there and she knew that George and Angus would be dying to know what happened between her and Daniel, but she couldn't face their questions. They'd want to know exactly what happened and what was said. No way was she going to tell them.

So once the dishes were done, Lola headed outside into the garden. There was a lot that needed doing and the day was warm and sunny. A perfect time to be outdoors.

By the middle of the afternoon it was too hot to work any longer. She stood and stretched her back. The garden was looking good and she'd made great progress in the vegetable garden, including starting a new bed.

She'd only had two vegetable beds until now but it was never enough. Eventually she'd like to have four or even five beds. That way she could keep planting and rotating all year to get a better yield. She loved to eat fresh from the garden.

Today there was not much to harvest so she'd leave it till the weekend and eat out tonight

Today was Thursday so cafés and restaurants wouldn't be as busy as they would be on Friday and Saturday nights.

Lola headed for the shower then dressed in long pants, a white blouse and a patterned, long waistcoat that she'd made a few days ago.

The white blouse was her own creation too but she'd had it for a while. The waistcoat though was new and she'd made it to go with the blouse and pants.

She'd found the cotton fabric in a shop in a small country town up in the Sunshine Coast Hinterland, which was about an hour and a half drive from where she lived in the city suburb.

She enjoyed going to small out-of-the-way places because they were so different and unique.

The fabric was gorgeous and was embroidered cotton. Not cheap, but good quality and perfect for the waist coat which came down over her hips and she wore it open with her blouse untucked.

She surveyed herself in the mirror before leaving the house. She loved the way her outfit looked. It looked good on her slim body and the dark colours in the embroidery contrasted well with her shoulder-length dark hair.

She travelled by train into the city because she wanted to have a glass or two of wine with her meal so didn't want to drink and drive.

The afternoon was still warm and sunny because it was Spring. A perfect time of year before the long, hot, humid months of summer.

In Brisbane, the only cold months were June, July and August, which were the winter months. But even then the temperature rarely dipped below twenty degrees during the day, but the nights were chilly.

Now it was the middle of Spring so it was perfect without being too hot.

In the city it was busy with workers trying to get home.

Lola walked through the crowded streets and over the bridge to the south bank which was a paradise of walkways, parks, cafés and markets.

There was also the lagoon with a man-made beach and it was next to a water park where children were running and screaming through all the squirting up and cascading down water features.

Lola loved the south bank of the city because it was so beautiful there and everyone always seemed to be having fun.

She wandered along the walkways under the arches covered in climbing plants and flowers, to a café called Steam. She liked this one the best because it looked out over a park area which was by the Brisbane River.

The café seating was under cover with only a low stone wall separating the tables from people passing by on the path between the café and the park.

Lola ordered her food and paid for it at the counter and was given a table number which was a white number painted on a black card attached to the top of a small metal stand. She was also given her glass of wine and she took both items to a table.

She chose a table with four chairs, two at each side, which was next to the wall so that she could sit and watch the world go by.

She put the small metal stand at the end of the table so that it could be easily seen and sat in a chair next to the wall.

After what seemed like only a minute or two her salad and garlic bread was brought to her table.

She ate slowly, enjoying her food and sipping her wine. It was so pleasant and relaxing just to sit there and people watch.

After her meal she went back to the counter and bought a second glass of wine and sipped it as the sun went down. It was fascinating to watch all the lights come on around the south bank and in the city across the river, as the day transformed into night.

The people sitting on the grass and passing by on the footpath were a mix of singles, couples, groups of friends and families.

She mainly watched the couples, feeling a little envious that she wasn't here as a couple too, with Daniel beside her.

It would be great if they could go out in public like other couples instead of hiding in her house or in places far away so that they wouldn't be recognised.

If only he was free so that they could come into the city and enjoy a meal together without the fear of being seen.

She thought about it some more, imagining them here together, laying on the beach at the lagoon soaking up the afternoon sun before heading to a nearby restaurant for dinner.

People she knew would stop as they passed by and she'd introduce Daniel to them and soon the two of them would be known as a couple. Everyone would know that they belonged together.

Damn it! That was it! That was what she wanted. She wanted the freedom of having a normal relationship with him instead of being hidden from view as if she was his dirty secret.

That was what was missing. Openness. It wasn't about whether she wanted to live with him or not, she just wanted to have a normal relationship with him.

As she sat and finished her wine, she watched other couples enjoying the freedom of being able to be together whenever they wanted and where ever they wanted.

If only she could enjoy that freedom too.

But the only way to stay with Daniel was to stay his secret.

*

Lola was so happy to have Daniel back in her life again. But at the same time, now that she realised it was the secretive way they always met that she didn't like, she felt aware of it all the more.

The only people that knew about their relationship were her staff. The only reason that it didn't matter was because they rarely saw him and they didn't know that he was married.

She tried to ignore how much being a secret bothered her. But now that she knew it, she felt like a dog with a bone and couldn't stop gnawing at it. She even started making small hints about it all the time.

When Daniel asked 'What shall we do this afternoon?' she said 'Let's go out for a walk.'

'You know we can't do that.'

'Oh yeah. You can't be seen with me in public.'

And when he asked 'Where do you want to go for dinner?' she said 'I know a great little café on the south bank.'

She could tell that her little digs were making him uncomfortable, but she just couldn't help it.

Every time she did it, she promised herself she wouldn't do it again. Then she would.

After a few weeks she couldn't stand it any longer. It was time to confront him.

She wanted him to understand how she felt. She wasn't even sure what response she was hoping for, but she knew she had to tell him. She didn't want to be his secret any more.

She wanted more than that. Damn it! She *deserved* more than that.

It would be a difficult confrontation. She knew that. It took her a few more days to build up the courage to tell him. But eventually she was ready.

The next time she saw him, she would tell him.

Chapter 4

Daniel came over on Saturday and he and Lola spent a wonderful afternoon together.

It began with a lunch, which mostly comprised a salad which they picked and prepared straight from the garden.

They lingered over their food with a chilled glass of white wine out on the back patio.

They moved to the sofa swing to finish their wine before going inside to the bedroom.

Their lovemaking was slow and tender.

Daniel undressed her slowly as she stood beside the bed, kissing and caressing each part of her body as it was exposed.

She undressed him in a similar way, hearing his groans of pleasure as her lips and tongue worked their way to the more intimate parts of his body.

They laid down on the bed together exploring each other in more different ways, until it all became too intense and they couldn't wait any longer.

As he entered her they both let out a cry of excitement.

Afterwards, they both lay on their backs in silence for a long time, too exhausted to speak. Lola felt lethargic from an overwhelming feeling of satisfaction.

Eventually they each showered and dressed.

Lola made coffee in a French press which they took out to the patio and they sat at the table.

The afternoon was warm and sunny and they could hear neighbourhood sounds of lawn mowers, children playing and dogs barking. But there was little sound from Lola's garden and no one could see them through the trees and tall bushes. It was so wonderful to sit here and enjoy time with Daniel. But at the same time, she still hated being his secret.

It was time to approach the subject.

She didn't know how to begin or what to say. After giving it a few minutes thought she said 'I don't want to be your secret. I want to be able to have a normal relationship where we go out in public and have mutual friends who know us as a couple.'

She stared out across the garden as she spoke, not able to look at him.

He made no immediate response. She waited, not daring to turn her head to see the expression on his face.

The silence felt heavy.

She heard him place his cup on the table. This was not good news. It was a sign he was leaving.

Out of the corner of her eye she saw him stand up.

Oh God. What had she done?

He let out a sigh. 'I've tried to make you understand. I care too much about my wife to hurt her. She needs me and I won't let her down. 'If she finds out about us it will hurt her, very much. I can't do that to her. 'If you want us to stay together then it has to be *this* way. Things must stay the way they are.

'Or not at all.'

He turned and walked back into the house. After a few seconds she heard the front door open and close.

Damn it! She hadn't wanted him to leave. She wanted him to understand exactly what it was like for her to be kept hidden all the time while he went home to his wife every time.

She wanted to come to some kind of compromise. But what? In their situation was there a compromise?

If she was honest with herself, what she really wanted was for Daniel to be single so that they could have a normal relationship.

Instead he always chose his wife over her. He always insisted that his wife needed him. Why couldn't he see that she needed him too? What was so special about his wife that he would always stand by her and would never hurt her? Did she have some sort of hold over him?

Lola shook her head as she picked up the coffee things and took them inside.

Daniel had made his decision to not be with Lola if it meant hurting his wife.

Now she had a decision to make too.

Chapter 5

After Daniel walked out on their idyllic Saturday afternoon together, the next few days seemed to drag on.

Lola hated this situation in their relationship. She wanted things to change and he didn't He would refuse to leave or hurt his wife in any way and instead would leave Lola. She knew that he would never choose her over his wife.

So she had made a decision. She wasn't going to let their relationship continue the way it was any more. Daniel was always adamant that things stayed this way or not at all. So she now chose not at all. But it wasn't easy. In fact is was damn hard to even think about it.

They'd been together for over two years so it would be hard to get used to life without him.

But used to it was what she needed to be, and the only way to do that was to live it. She had to simply carry on her life without him. So far it had been less than a week yet it felt like much more than that. Time seemed to be dragging.

Lola had kept herself busy. She'd spent a couple of days working in the garden, putting her hands to the soil as much as possible in the hopes that enough "grounding" would help keep her spirits up.

She also spent more time than usual at the shop and spent her evenings sitting out on the back patio with her sewing machine, making herself some new clothes for summer while listening to some audio books on her MP3 player.

Her life was busy, but without Daniel it also felt empty. It almost felt as though she was simply going through the motions of being busy, when what she was really doing, was passing time until she saw him again.

By the following Saturday she was missing him a lot. It was only the previous weekend that she last saw him but it already felt like weeks ago.

She wondered if he felt the same way. Was he sitting at home reminiscing about their last afternoon together? Or was he otherwise occupied, having a lovely time with his wife?

Either way it shouldn't matter anymore. She didn't want to see him if it meant that nothing would change and he'd always go home to the wife who *needed* him more than she did.

What she wanted now was time, because it was the thing that was supposed to heal all wounds. And at the moment she did feel wounded because being without him hurt. It made her heart ache.

But she was always strong when she needed to be, and she needed to be strong now. She was determined to get used to the separation.

The best thing was to keep busy so that she didn't have time to think about it.

It was now only 10 o'clock in the morning and she had the whole day to get through.

It was time to go to work. She'd get changed and go and work in the shop today.

*

When she arrived it was busy. There were several groups of customers in the shop.

George looked up at her and smiled as she walked in the door. He also looked slightly surprised to see her again too. She'd been there almost every day that week. But he was busy serving someone so didn't have time to speak.

Susan was also working and was busy helping a woman try on different earrings. Susan was a single mother and her daughter, Chloe, came to work with her when school was closed.

On seeing Susan, Lola's eyes quickly scanned the shop. Sure enough, there was the ten year old behind the counter, sitting on a stool reading a book.

'Hi Chloe,' she said as she put her handbag on a shelf behind the counter.

Chloe looked up and smiled. 'Hi Lola. Look I've borrowed this really great book from the library all about serial killers." She held up the cover for Lola to see.

'Creepy.'

'No, it's great,' and immediately went back to being engrossed in her book.

Lola went through the door next to where Chloe sat, into the back room to get a cup of coffee.

She could hear a voice coming through the wall of the tarot reading room. 'I'm seeing a uniform. It's a man who wears a uniform. Is it a police uniform or a military uniform?'

It was Lindsay, their freelance tarot card reader who was always a big hit at the weekends.

Lola picked up the jug of coffee from the coffee machine and poured herself a cup.

'So what's going on?'

Lola turned to look at George. She hadn't heard him come in. 'With what?' she asked him.

'With you. We don't usually see this much of you all week.'

'Complaining?'

'Hell no,' George laughed. 'It's always great to see you. But it's how much we're seeing of you and not him.'

'It's only a week since I saw him.'

'But still...'

Lola laughed. 'Sticky beak.'

'It's just that I care so much,' said George, putting his arm around her shoulders and squeezing her tight.

Lola smiled and shrugged away from him. 'Well care less, will you.' She picked up her cup of coffee and carried it past him back out into the shop adding 'sticky beak' as she went.

'But a caring sticky beak,' she heard him call from behind and it made her smile again.

Susan was just finishing with her earring customer as she handed the woman her receipt. To Lola she said, 'It's been really busy this morning. We haven't stopped.'

'Good. It must be the nice weather that's bringing everyone out.'

'I don't know what it is but even Lindsay's been flat out and has had a queue of people waiting for readings. One of them is over there still waiting for his turn.'

Lola looked in the direction Susan gestured to where a man stood leafing through one of the self-help books.

She felt her heart skip a beat as just for a split second she thought it was Daniel. But it wasn't. The blonde hair and short stocky build were where the similarities ended.

Thank goodness it wasn't him. She didn't know what she'd say if he did walk in.

She just had to hope that he didn't. Although her aching heart still wished that he would.

Chapter 6

One week dragged into three and still no sign of Daniel. Lola was sad in one way but glad in another. Sad that their relationship was over but glad that she could now get on with her life without him.

She did miss him in some ways but she figured that was only natural because he had been such a large part of her life. Her feelings were mixed between her head saying no and her heart saying yes.

Thankfully she had her own busy life to get on with which would help her to move on and forget him, because that was what she was determined to do.

She'd spent a lot of time at work lately discussing expansions for the business.

She'd decided to make the back room smaller to make the shop floor bigger, delete slow-selling items, carry more different lines of stock and change their system of ordering so that they didn't have as much stock in the back room.

She had a builder designing plans for the physical changes and an IT consultant changing her online database system of stock to include the new lines and change the frequency of stock ordering.

All this would change things dramatically. Customers loved to come in and browse and soon there would be a larger shop with more to look at. And the back room, although smaller, would be more of a staff room, a pleasant place to sit and take a break rather than a small table surrounded by boxes in a big room.

During the alterations she would keep the shop open as long as possible but she knew she would have to close for a week or two while the major alterations were done and the shop was re-stocked.

With all the changes going on it had made it easier for her to try and forget about Daniel and move on with her life.

She must have been right about needing time to help heal her wounds because she had never felt so strong or confident about their relationship being finished.

She was finally over him.

Or so she thought. But the following Monday changed her mind.

*

Lola came into work on Monday morning because the builder wanted to go over the final plans with her before he submitted them to the city council for building approval.

The builder showed up shortly after 9.30 and he and Lola spent nearly an hour discussing the changes and the timeline of how it was all going to be done.

When he left she decided to have a coffee break, but after spending so long in the back room she decided to take a break.

'George, I'm just going out for a coffee. I'm not going far so I won't be long.'

'Our company not good enough for you anymore?' he asked with a smile.

'I'm just sick of the sight of the back room this morning and I could do with some fresh air.' She made air quotes with her fingers as she said "fresh" because in the middle of the city the air always smelled of car exhaust fumes.

George laughed as she turned and left the shop.

She'd planned to go to one of the nearby cafés and thought she'd stroll past a few and find one which wasn't too busy.

It felt good to be out walking so she changed her mind and decided to walk a few streets further and go somewhere else.

After about ten minutes she found a small café that had plenty of tables outside and most of them were empty.

Inside were many more tables, most of them occupied by people in work suits having out-of-office meetings or working on their laptop computers.

She went to the counter at the back and ordered a black coffee.

'I want to sit outside and drink it but I'd like it in a takeaway cup so that I can take it with me when I leave.'

'Sure,' the young barista said and immediately picked up a cardboard coffee cup.

She opened her handbag and took out her purse ready to pay.

From the table to the left she heard a man laugh.

She froze. Daniel!

'I don't believe it,' he said.

For a split second she thought he was talking to her. Then she heard a woman's voice. 'It's true. I couldn't believe it either at first. Thought it was some sort of joke, but he was serious.' Then they both laughed together.

Lola turned her head slightly to see them. They were sitting at a small table for two. Daniel had his back to her and the woman was sitting opposite him. What a relief that he hadn't seen her.

The woman was an attractive brunette and judging by Daniel's reaction he was really enjoying her company. She carried on laughing and telling her funny story, but Lola didn't hear what she was saying. She was too busy studying their body language. They were obviously very comfortable in each other's company and the realisation dawned on her.

This must be Daniel's wife.

She watched them some more, trying not to stare but they were so engrossed in each other that they didn't notice her, or notice anyone else in the place for that matter.

The woman said something to Daniel. He leaned forward and patted her hand on the table.

She patted the top of his hand with her other hand and then they both picked up their cups.

'That's $3.95 thanks.'

Lola paid for her coffee and left. She didn't sit outside with it as she'd planned. She didn't want Daniel and his wife to come out and see her.

Instead she hurried to Anzac Square and sat on the grass under a bottle tree.

She sat wither legs and cradled her coffee cup between them. She hung her head so that her hair obscured her face and quietly wept.

There were a lot of people in the park and she didn't want any of them to see her cry. People in Brisbane were usually quite kind, even to strangers, and would always try and help anyone who was upset or distressed. She didn't want anyone to ask her what was wrong because she didn't even know herself.

She thought that she was over Daniel but obviously she wasn't. And seeing him with his wife, hurt.

Or maybe it wasn't his wife. Maybe it was a relative or a work colleague or a friend.

She realised that she had no idea who his friends, colleagues and relatives were. In fact, she knew almost nothing about his life.

He didn't like to talk about his life because he preferred to keep his relationship with Lola completely separate and that meant never involving her in his "other" life.

But the way he'd touched the woman's hand in the café meant that she was almost certainly his wife. Surely he wouldn't touch a work colleague that way?

'It must have been his wife,' she told herself again.

Ha! His wife! Lola let out a small laugh, which stopped her tears. She knew so little about Daniel that she didn't even know the woman's name. They had only ever mentioned her as his wife. No name.

Maybe her name was Lola and that's why he never mentioned it. She laughed to herself again, and began to feel better.

How embarrassing to have a breakdown like this in public. She took a tissue out of her bag, wiped her eyes, blew her nose, looked up and tucked her hair back behind her ears. It felt good to feel air on her face and she needed it to clear away all signs of crying.

She sat and sipped her coffee as she rationally looked back over what she'd seen in the café and how she'd reacted.

Seeing Daniel with another woman had negatively impacted on her emotions straight away. Regardless of who the woman was, Lola had felt jealous. It was plain and simple. She didn't like seeing Daniel with another woman.

A new thought suddenly struck her. What if she wasn't just another woman, but was "the" other woman in his life now? What if he'd moved on an found someone else in his life?

It was possible but she didn't think this woman was new to him because she had the feeling that the two of them were quite used to being together. Theirs was not a new relationship. And one thing she also knew was that Daniel would never be seen out in public with his mistress.

She had probably been right in the first place and the woman was his wife - 'with no name,' she thought sarcastically to herself.

One thing was for sure though, this unexpected meeting had proven to her that she wasn't over Daniel yet.

And if she was honest with herself, she never would be.

The problem though, was what was she going to do about it?

Chapter 7

By Friday she could take it no longer. She knew that Daniel finished work early on Fridays because he would often meet her at the shop at around 2.30 so she figured he must finish around two.

So she waited outside his building, across the road, sitting on a low brick wall. She wasn't even sure if he'd come out that way but she was pretty certain that he would.

Sure enough, just after 2 o'clock, people began to pour out of the building. It was a tall block of offices that dwarfed some of the skyscrapers around it.

She scanned the crowds as hundreds of people came through the front doors and headed off in different directions.

Soon she saw him. He walked out, talking with another man. They stopped to talk for a few minutes and then headed in different directions.

She stood up and followed him, still staying on her side of the road. It didn't take long for him to look across and see her.

He tried not to look surprised but clearly he was. Without looking at her again, he turned down the next side street.

She walked to the next intersection, crossed over at the traffic lights and walked back to the side street.

The street wasn't very long and Daniel was about halfway down, standing in a shop doorway.

When she caught up to him, they slowly carried on walking down the street together, then along the street at the bottom, and back up to the main road again, talking as they went.

Lola started talking first as they walked.

'I need to see you.'

'What for?'

'Because I want to see you.'

'I don't think there's anything more we can say.'

'Do you miss me?'

Daniel was silent for a few seconds before he answered. 'Every day.'

'I miss you every day too.'

'But the usual problem remains.'

'I need to see you. Come round, please?'

There was another silence.

'OK. I'll be there in an hour or two.'

By now they were nearly at the main road again. Daniel quickly picked up his pace and walked off on his own.

She felt rejected the way he didn't want to be seen with her, but at least he'd agreed to see her, and soon, which was a good sign.

Or was it?

*

Lola went home and showered and changed and waited nervously for Daniel to arrive.

After a while the doorbell rang and she let him in. He looked just as nervous as she felt.

They went out onto the patio where she had a pitcher of Sangria. She was already drinking a glass and she poured one for him.

He took it without saying a word and they sat on the sofa swing together.

'Daniel, I was wrong.'

'About what?'

'About being a secret. I was looking for a compromise in our situation but I've realised there isn't one. Not if you want to stay with your wife.

He turned to look at her.

'Lola, there's something that you really, *really* need to understand. I will never *ever* leave my wife. Nor will I *ever* do anything to jeopardize my marriage. That's why we can never be seen together.

'And not only that, the time I spend with you must *never* cross over with the rest of my life. The two must stay completely separate.

'I don't talk about you with the other people in my life and I won't talk about the other people with you either. So you can never ask me about what I do when I'm not with you.

'That's the only way that it can work. Otherwise I'd get conversations mixed up and I'd forget whether I said something to you or someone else from the other part of my life.

'So if you and I are going to have a future together, then that's the way it has to be.

'So when I'm with you it's never anywhere that I spend time with other people. We can't be seen together and we can't go to places around here. I know that this isn't the way you want things to be, but it's the way it HAS to be.'

Lola understood perfectly. It wasn't what she wanted but she had no choice if she wanted to be with Daniel.

'I know. And you're right. It's not the way I want things to be but if it's the only way then I'll take it. I don't want to be without you.'

'I don't want to be without you either. This past few weeks has been hell.'

She wanted to scream at him, 'It didn't look like hell when you were in the coffee shop the other day having a great time with your wife!' But instead she said, 'It's been worse for me. I actually started going to work every day.'

He laughed. 'That's not like you at all.'

'It gets even worse. I also started plans to expand the business.'

'Oh my God. You really have been suffering.' And with that he laughed again, took her hand and led her into the bedroom, leaving their glasses on the table as they went.

Their lovemaking seemed insatiable after such a long absence. She was hungry for his body and he was equally hungry for hers.

And it felt damn good.

Chapter 8

Lola was really happy to be back with Daniel and was so busy with her business changes at the same time that the weeks just flew by.

Then she had a couple of quieter weeks when she had to close the shop so that the major work of moving the back wall could be carried out.

She spent most of this time at home, working in the garden. She also spent this new free time reflecting on her relationship with Daniel.

She had accepted his terms, although she was far from happy about them. She wanted to be able to say things like 'How's work?' but he had made it quite clear that these subjects were taboo.

So now she knew she couldn't even ask him if the woman he was with in the coffee shop was his wife. But naturally she as dying to know. If it was his wife then it was strange that they seemed to be so happy together like any normal couple.

When Daniel told her that he and his wife hadn't had sex for years, she assumed it was because they were unhappily married. But now she'd seen them together she knew that her assumption wasn't true.

But how could two people live together happily as a couple if they had no sex life? It seemed like some weird type of cult thing. 'You can be married but you must never give in to the temptation of lust and sins of the flesh.' Weird!

Or maybe they were just content with not having sex.

No. That couldn't be true, otherwise Daniel wouldn't be having sex with someone else. He'd be happily celibate.

Whatever his marital arrangement was, Lola was just happy that they were back together, even if he wouldn't compromise in any way.

Seeing him so happy with his wife still rankled her though. She didn't want them to be happy together. She wanted them to be miserable because she didn't like to think that he was happy being with another woman when he wasn't with her.

Her only hope of stopping it from bothering her was the possibility that she was wrong and the woman wasn't his wife.

But then, who was she?

The only way to find out was to ask Daniel but there was no way that he would tell her. He'd probably just get angry that she asked him about his "other" life.

He'd talk about anything else with her. His childhood, favourite things, movies, holiday places and even his bucket list. But never, ever would he discuss other people in his life, his job or his family. The only reason he couldn't hide his place of work from her was because he often was wearing the company logo on the front of his shirt when he met her after work.

So it had now come down to his way or the highway. And his rules were strict.

Not hurting his wife was important to him for reasons he would never divulge. Perhaps it was because he was a caring person, which wasn't really a bad thing. It was actually a quality she admired in him. He wouldn't even step on ants.

She'd made the decision to stay with him because seeing him on his terms was better than not seeing him at all. Three agonizing weeks without him had proved to her that she needed him in her life.

And being with him a few hours a week on his terms was far better than not seeing him at all.

So now she felt content.

Except...who was that woman?

Chapter 9

Lola lay in the crook of his arm. Sex had been great as usual and now they both lay naked in bed in the afterglow.

'I missed this so much when I didn't see you for a few weeks.' He gave her an affectionate squeeze as he spoke.

Lola snuggled closer. 'I missed you too. This is a big lonely bed for one.'

She decided that if there was ever a good opportunity to bring up seeing him in the coffee shop, this was it.

'Strangely enough, I did actually see you in the city one day during that time.'

'I don't remember seeing you.'

'You didn't.'

'Were you walking behind me?'

'No. You were sitting down.'

'How do you know I didn't see you then?'

'You had your back to me. But your wife was facing me. She saw me.'

Daniel moved his arm out from around her and half sat up to look at her, leaning on one elbow.

'My wife?' He sounded annoyed.

'Well, it was a woman and the way you touched her I figured it must be your wife.'

'Whoa! Back up. What woman? Where did you see us?'

Lola held the sheet over her breast with her underarms as she too sat half up and propped herself on one elbow so that she could look him in the face and see his reactions.

'In a coffee shop in the city. I went in to buy a coffee and the two of you were sitting at a table near the counter.'

'And I touched her?'

'You put your hand on top of hers on the table.'

'How long were you watching us?'

'Just long enough to get my coffee. Geez! It's a public place. I went in for coffee, not to spy on you. I didn't even know you were there until I heard your voice.' Now she was getting annoyed. He seemed to be defensive.

'Sorry.' His shoulders lowered as he said it. She hadn't even noticed that he'd tensed up. In a calmer voice he said, 'For the record, she is not my wife.'

'Who is she?'

This time she saw him go tense. 'It doesn't matter who she is. I don't want to talk about other people in my life. I've told you that before. I thought you understood.'

'Jesus Christ, Daniel!' Her voice was raised. She got out of bed and began picking her clothes up off the floor. 'What the hell is wrong with you? I see you out with someone and ask who they are and you get shitty about it.

'For goodness sake! I know you have your "rules" about taboo subjects, but it was just a *normal* question like *normal* couples ask each other.

'Sometimes you take your ridiculous rules *too* far.' And with that she carried her clothes to the bathroom.

When she came out, Daniel was dressed and sitting on the edge of the bed staring out the window.

He turned to look at her. 'I know you don't like the way things are but I have my reasons. I will tell you that the woman is a relative of mine. A blood relation.'

She stared at him. 'I know all about your rules and reasons, but bloody hell. If I see you out and about with someone and ask who it was it's no reason to get angry with me. We do both work in the same city so sometimes we are going to run into each other.

'And now it seems that you've introduced a new rules. So now not only can I not talk about your life when your not with me, but I'm not allowed to talk about your life when you *are* with me if someone else is there too.'

'I'm sorry.'

'I don't want your apologies. Just go.'

As he left the room he said, 'I'll be back in a few days.'

Right there and then she didn't care if she saw him again or not.

But in her heart she knew that in a few days she'd be glad to see him again.

She just hoped the argument was over.

Chapter 10

True to his word, Daniel returned three days later, on Friday afternoon.

Lola had been at work all day looking at all the alterations that had been done and discussing the last minute jobs such as painting and the new shop fittings that would still take a few more days to complete.

She arrived home in the middle of the afternoon and headed straight for the shower. It was a hot day and the shop was dirty so she thought she'd shower first and then have an early dinner because she'd missed lunch.

Daniel arrived just as she went into the kitchen.

'Hi,' she greeted him happily at the door, hoping that he was glad to see her and wouldn't mention their last argument. But straight away she could tell that his visit wasn't social.

'Lola, we need to talk.'

She closed the door and led him into the kitchen. 'No we don't need to talk at all. What you really mean is that you're going to talk and I have to obey everything you say. That is, of course, unless you've come to apologise.'

'For what?'

'For getting angry over nothing. Gee Daniel, who was that woman you were having coffee with? Was it your wife? How dare you ask me questions!' She spoke in a mocking tone as she condensed their last conversation.

His face flushed red with anger. 'It wasn't like that.'

'Er...excuse me? It was *exactly* like that. I asked a question and you got angry and left.'

'If I ask you not to talk about the other people in my life can't you just respect that?'

'You mean, can't I do as I'm told?'

'No. I mean have some respect for my feelings.'

I *did* have respect for your feelings. Do you want to know how I did that? By not coming over and saying hello to you when you were with someone else.'

They stared angrily at each other.

'Just don't ever ask me about my wife.'

'What? She who is such a secret that I'm not even allowed to know her name. That wife?'

'This isn't funny.'

'Do I look like I'm laughing?'

'You're ridiculing everything.'

'That's because it's ridiculous! I see you with another woman and say, "Was that your wife?" and boom! Here we are having not one, but now *two* arguments about it.'

Daniel took a deep breath and attempted to speak calmly. 'I don't want to keep arguing about it. What's past is past. So let's agree to drop it. And please don't talk about my wife. OK?'

'Why?'

'Stop it.'

'No. I'm serious. Why?'

'I said I don't want to keep going over this.'

'We're not. You said you didn't want to talk about the past. I'm talking about things I'm not allowed to say in the future. Why are you so petty when it comes to your wife?'

'I'm not kidding. If we can't stop it, it's over. I won't come back.'

'Threats now? If she means that much to you then why are you an unfaithful husband?'

'This is over. Goodbye Lola.' He turned and left.

As he went she yelled 'Next time I see you out with another woman I'll ask *her* if she's your wife. That way I'm not breaking the rules and asking *you*!'

His only reply was slamming the door.

Chapter 11

Lola decided that enough was enough. If Daniel was so protective of his wife then she could have him. It was time to move on.

It would have been easy to get in touch with him and ask for forgiveness and promise to never mention his wife again, but damn it! Why should she?

Their Breakups were happening too often now and he always blamed her. But she hadn't done anything wrong.

Daniel had said that he was leaving for good this time, so maybe it was for the best. Maybe it was time to let go. After more than two years together it wouldn't be easy, but she'd do it.

The next couple of weeks passed quickly. The building work was finished, the shop was cleaned and re-stocked and the doors opened for business once again. She enjoyed being there and seeing how all the new changes worked.

Without the big storage room, stock now had to be put out on display immediately but with having a bigger shop, and letting stock run down more, it all worked quite well, even if it did take a bit of getting used to.

On the third week of the shop re-opening, she went in on Monday morning to make sure for one last time that everything was running smoothly.

She let the staff take care of the customers while she sat at the table in the back room and went over the recent figures to see if there'd been any change in trade and to her delight, trade had been more brisk and profits were up. Not bad in just two weeks.

She thought it might have taken a while for things to settle down once they re-opened but apparently it hadn't. Instead the alterations had an immediate, positive effect.

By 11a.m. she'd had enough and decided it was time to leave.

She put the computer away and spoke briefly with George and Angus before picking up her handbag from behind the counter and heading out the door.

She had intended to go straight home, but it was such a beautiful day that she decided to enjoy a leisurely coffee first.

There was a café nearby with plenty of outside tables so she headed over there.

'Hey, nice to see you again,' the barista greeted her when she got to the counter.

She couldn't help but smile because he seemed so genuinely happy.

She was somewhat of a regular customer here so had seen the guy many times. He was about her age, in his early thirties, was quite attractive and when he smiled he had two deep dimples in his cheeks that made him look rather boyish.

'Thanks. Can I have...'

He put up his hand to silence her. 'I know. A regular, long black, in a take-out cup that you can drink here first and take it with you when you go.'

'Ah. You're not just good making coffee, you're a mind reader too.'

'No. I just have a good memory.'

'Of course.'

'Go and sit down. I'll bring it to you.'

'Thanks.' She placed the exact change on the counter and went back outside to sit down.

The café was busy and there were only three empty tables left outside. One of them was smaller and only had two chairs so she chose that one.

It felt like she'd only just sat down when her coffee was placed on he table in front of her.

'There you go.'

'Thanks.' She looked up as she spoke and saw the dimpled barista smiling at her.

'Just on your way to work?' he asked.

'No, I've just finished for the day.'

'Wow. You must have started early.'

She laughed. 'Good grief, no. I've just finished everything I needed to do already, so no point staying any longer than I need to.'

'You must have an understanding boss.'

'Yeah, I do. She's the best. And so smart too. They say you can't have brains and good looks, but she definitely has both.'

'Let me guess. You ARE the boss,' he laughed.

'It's one of the many hats I wear at work.'

'Where do you work?'

'Cheriton Charms.'

'That new age, hippy shop?'

'Well, I wouldn't describe it that way, but yes.'

'I've been in there a few times but I've never seen you in there.'

'I try not to work too often,' she joked.

His mood suddenly seemed to change. He looked down thoughtfully at his feet for a few seconds.

When he looked up again he wasn't smiling anymore and his dimples had gone.

'Look, I don't want to be too forward or presumptuous, but do you fancy going out for a drink sometime?'

She was taken completely by surprise by the question. She hadn't expected him to say anything like that. She was silent for a few seconds while she thought about it.

It had never crossed her mind to date the guy from the café. But why not? He seemed decent enough and what could it hurt?

'Sure. Why not?'

His smile and dimples returned instantly. 'Great! How about dinner instead of just drinks? I could book us a table somewhere for Saturday night.'

She wasn't too sure about letting him choose the restaurant. She preferred casual places to eat and was worried that he might try and impress her by booking somewhere too fancy.

'How about if we meet in the city and take a walk over to the south bank. There's plenty of places to eat there so we can take our pick.'

He was agreeable immediately, so they arranged to meet in Anzac Square.

Lola finished her coffee and headed home feeling quite excited. It was ages since she'd had a first date and she felt like a teenager again.

It was also a long time since she'd been out in public with a man so she was really looking forward to it.

Sadly the evening was a disaster.

*

It began well. They both arrived in Anzac Square at the same time. Walking over to the south bank they laughed when they realised that they didn't even know each other's name, so they did formal introductions.

His name was Rory. Lola wasn't sure if she liked his name, but as it turned out, it was the least unpleasant thing about him.

She guided him to her favourite eatery, Steam. Rory complained that it wasn't what he called a "proper" restaurant.

She tried to get him to explain what he meant and he ranted and raved about no walls, no service, no cloth napkins and no menus brought to the table.

And if that wasn't bad enough, it was worse when their food arrived.

He seemed to think that it wasn't "presented" well enough, but to Lola it just looked like food.

Then when he began to eat, she couldn't believe the noise he made. He cut up his food into tiny pieces and noisily sucked them off his fork and into his mouth. Then he ate with small, fast, lip-smacking, sounds. And he did it with every bite - every small bit. He cut his food up so tiny that it was *a lot* of small, sucking bites.

She couldn't eat her own food because the noise he was making was disgusting, and other people were staring. She felt so embarrassed. Rory also talked with food in his mouth.

When she thought about it afterwards, she should have left the table and run home. But instead, she politely stayed and suffered through the entire meal.

After they'd eaten he asked if she wanted another drink. She didn't. She just wanted to get away from him. He tried to insist on taking her home but she flatly refused.

They walked back over the bridge again and he talked the whole time. He put his arm around her as they walked which made their hips press together. She had the urge to bolt the whole time.

Back in Anzac Square, he finally let go of her.

'Well here we are. Are you sure you don't want me to take you home?'

'Oh absolutely.'

'How are you going to get there?'

'It's not that far so I'll probably walk.'

'In the city? At night?'

'It's Brisbane. It's safe.'

'If you're sure'. He put his hands on her hips and turned her to face him He then embraced her and tried to kiss her at the same time.

She couldn't help herself. She put her hand on his chest and pushed him back. 'Whoa, Romeo.' She tried to laugh.

'What's up?'

'It just seems weird, you know? One minute you're serving me coffee and now here we are in the park at night.'

'It's not weird, really. We've been together for hours getting to know each other.' he bent his head down towards her face and tried to kiss her again, but she leaned away.

'What's wrong?' He sounded annoyed.

'I just didn't realise it was this sort of date, you know? I thought it would be more like friends, or two people who know each other having a meal together, just spending time together.'

He dropped his hands down by his sides with a loud slap. 'Fine. OK. See you later, friend,' and he turned and walked away. He was trying to look angry but instead he just seemed sulky. Lola didn't really care how he looked. She was simply relieved that he'd gone.

She walked home with a spring in her step. It felt so good to be away from him. Away from the noisy food sucker. What a weird way to eat. She wondered how many other women had been repulsed by his eating habits.

Yuck! He seemed so normal until then. But she guessed this was all part of being in the dating scene. You had to date a few bad guys before you could meet a decent one. She just hoped that she didn't have to date many bad ones. Fingers crossed.

Chapter 12

It was now well over a week since her disastrous date with Rory, and she hadn't been in the café where he worked since.

It wasn't that she was trying to avoid him. She just hadn't wanted to go there. But the whole time she had wondered if their meeting would be awkward when she finally did see him.

Well, today was the day.

She'd spent the morning working in the shop and now she was on her way to the café. She was determined to go in there and act casual as if nothing had changed and she hoped that he'd do the same.

Coffee wasn't even something that she wanted. She just wanted to face a potentially awkward moment to get it out of the way.

Now she was there. Most of the outside tables were taken so were most of the tables inside, but she had no intention of sitting inside. After taking an unconscious deep breath, she went in.

Rory was there, as usual, behind the counter with another guy who was also serving customers.

It was the other guy who looked up first as she approached. 'Yes? What can I get you?'

She opened her mouth to speak, but another voice spoke first.

'A regular long black in a takeaway cup that she wants to drink here.'

It was Rory speaking for her, smiling and showing his two huge dimples.

She smiled back at him, relieved that nothing had changed and he wasn't avoiding her.

To the guy serving her she said, 'Wasn't that clever? I said that without moving my lips.'

He laughed. 'That's $3.95 thanks.'

She took out her purse and handed him a $5 note. He gave her change and Rory made her coffee.

She carried her cup outside and sat at one of the empty tables.

It was another beautiful day. Hot if you were busy running around or out in the sun, but just right if you were sat in the shade like she was.

'Hi, Lola.' The voice startled her out of her reverie. She looked up. It was Lindsay, the tarot card reader from her shop.

'Oh, hi. Are you working today?'

'Yeah but not for another hour. I came to the city early because I had other things to do, but I finished sooner than I thought.'

'Get a coffee and join me.'

Lindsay looked hesitant. 'Are you sure? I don't want to interrupt you.'

'I'm finished for the day and have nowhere to go in a hurry so you're welcome to join me.'

'OK. Thanks.' She disappeared inside and returned a minute later with a frothy cup of coffee. 'It's not a bad place to sit is it?' she said as she placed her cup on the table and sat facing Lola.

'It's not bad, but I had another reason to choose this place.'

'How so?'

Lola told her about her date with Rory and his weird noisy eating habits.

They both ended up laughing loudly as Lola tried to imitate his actions.'

'I'll tell you what,' said Lindsay. "Why don't you and I go out this Saturday? I know a place that's great to go and sit and drink and quite a few cute guys go there too so you might meet someone with better manners. Who knows?'

'Oh I don't know. My last date has put me off for a long time.'

'No. It's like riding a horse. You need to get straight back up and try again.'

Lola thought about it for a moment and decided that there was really nothing to think about. She liked Lindsay and she had no other plans for Saturday night.

'OK. Why not? If nothing else we can go out and have a few drinks and a laugh.'

'Now you're talking my language.'

They made arrangements to meet in the city and walk to Lindsay's bar from there.

Lola spent the rest of the week looking forward to her night out.

She didn't have many friends. In fact, if she was honest, she didn't have any friends at all, at least, not in the sense that she had friends to go clubbing with. Having friends was not a priority on her list of "must have" things. In fact, they weren't even on her list.

Lola was someone who was happy in her own company. Naturally she liked talking to other people and she always did at work or when she was out shopping or doing other things. But she never had a need for friends that would come over for coffee or go out drinking with her.

That was probably why she was looking forward to a night out with Lindsay. It was something different that she didn't usually do, and she liked Lindsay.

On Saturday night she took her time to get ready and even had a long, leisurely bath, sitting and soaking for a long time.

Then she dried her hair, clipped it up with some rhinestone hair clips and put on her favourite red dress that was tight fitting without looking "slutty."

The shoes she wore were flat heeled so that she could walk into the city.

It was still daylight as she set off but was dark by the time she met up with Lindsay, who was dressed in a similar dress but hers was black.

The two women walked to the bar. It looked like just a plain brick building from the outside and was in a quiet alleyway. The door was solid wood that pulled outward.

As they entered, Lola's eyes quickly adjusted to the gloom. It was brighter than outside, but the walls, ceiling and upholstery were all black which made it look gloomy.

It was a large room with a bar in the centre, plenty of places to sit and a small dance floor and DJ at one far side.

The music wasn't loud so it was easy to speak.

'What would you like?' Lindsay asked.

'I'll have a schooner of beer. Heavy.' Lindsay herself ordered a glass of white wine.

They sat at a high table near the bar that had four high stools around it, two at each side. They sat opposite each other.

It felt so great to be out doing something different. Hell, it was great to be out in public for a change, which was something that never happened with Daniel. How great it would have been if they could have done this. Just come out into the city for a drink any time they wanted.

To Lindsay she said, 'This looks like a great place. How come I didn't know about it?'

'I think it's one of those places that only gets known by word of mouth. I'd been here quite a few times before I even knew what it was called.'

'What is it called?'

'Warren's Bar. Apparently there used to be another place with the same name but it closed down decades ago. This place is open till late every night which makes it a handy place to drop in and have a drink after a movie or a show.'

'Yeah, I like it,' said Lola feeling instantly at home.

Lindsay said, 'I was thinking about your disastrous date earlier and I remembered a bad date of my own once, but it was over ten years ago now.

Lola was intrigued and just knew it would be a funny story. 'Do tell.'

'Well, I met a guy in a bar but it was late and the place was closing and I'd had a few drinks but we agreed to meet up the following night at the same place.

I went back to meet him at the arranged time and for the life of me I couldn't remember anything about him but I did remember feeling attracted to him, although that might have only been because I was drunk and horny.'

Lola was grinning and couldn't wait to hear the rest of the story.

'Anyway, I went into the place hoping that I'd recognise him or that he'd recognise me if I didn't. Sure enough, he came straight up to me but in the sober light of day I thought he looked a little odd but I just couldn't put my finger on it. But he was really enthusiastic to see me and kept putting his arm around me and plied me with drinks.'

She stopped to sip her wine before carrying on.

'And then he said the darnedest thing and I thought, oh my God! That's it! That's why he looks so weird and the whole thing freaked me out. So I made up an excuse that I needed to go to the toilet and I ran away. I mean, literally. I ran down the street as fast as I could in case he saw me leaving and chased after me.'

'What did he say?' Lola was leaning forward in anticipation.

'No. It was more like, what did SHE say.'

Lola burst out laughing. 'No!'

'Yes! A big, fat, ugly, yes! It seems he/she was waiting for a sex change operation and so had been taking male hormones to deepen her voice and grow facial hair.

'The worst part was that apparently, I'd been told this the night before and I said I was OK with it. That's why he/she was so happy to see me. Thought she'd found someone who understood. Yeesh! Not me.'

They were still laughing when two men approached their table. 'Hi,' one of them said.

Lola hadn't seen them approaching. The one who spoke was an attractive man in his thirties (she guessed), slim and slightly taller than her.

'Mind if we sit down?' He gestured at the two empty stools.

'Help yourselves,' Lola told them. She and Lindsay exchanged raised eyebrows.

After introductions, it turned out that the two guys, James and Matt, worked in construction together and funnily enough, they worked for the same company as Daniel. But of course they didn't know him because they were labourers and worked on one of the sites whereas Daniel worked in the head office.

James was the one who'd spoken first and he and Lola had their eyes locked on each other the whole time. She barely noticed his friend.

The four of them sat chatting although it was Lola and James that did most of the talking.

Eventually Matt and Lindsay sat deep in conversation and James and Lola spoke at length too and they all had two more drinks.

Lola really liked James. He had a genuine smile, laughed a lot and seemed interested in everything she said.

He told her about his work.

She told him she worked at Cheriton Charms, but didn't mention that she owned the business. She never told people that because they didn't need to know.

When she finished her last drink, James offered to get her another but she declined and said she wanted to go home.

She and James took out their cell phones and exchanged numbers. They said goodbye outside and so did Matt and Lindsay.

They stood in the quiet alley. James with his arms around Lola and Matt with his arms around Lindsay.

James kissed her, long and passionately. It felt great, but at the same time, it felt foreign.

After kissing only Daniel for the last two years it felt strange to be in the arms of another man, kissing lips that she wasn't used to.

Eventually she broke the embrace and she and Lindsay said goodbye to their dates and walked out of the alley together.

They giggled like two schoolgirls once they got around the corner and thought they were out of earshot.

'We pulled!' announced Lindsay. 'Didn't see that one coming tonight. You seeing yours again?'

'Yeah. I got his number and he got mine.'

'Same here. Do you think we'll ever hear from them again?'

'Who knows?' And as she said it she also thought 'And I'm not even sure if I really care.'

Half of her wanted him to get in touch and the other half didn't.

Either way, she'd leave it up to the universe to decide.

If he asked her out again she'd go.

But if he didn't call, she wouldn't call him either.

Chapter 13

It was six weeks later. James did call the next day and they'd been dating ever since.

She really liked him. He was a nice guy and quite easy to get along with. Their relationship quickly became intimate and they slept together within the first few days.

Sex with James felt so strange at first. She was so used to Daniel's touch that she hadn't realised how comfortable sex had become with him, if comfortable was the right word.

With Daniel she had a routine and an understanding. They knew what each other liked and didn't like and knew instinctively if the other person was or wasn't "in the mood."

His touch was familiar and she thrilled every time he touched her. She could also relax into the moment because the familiarity between them made sex easy and therefore more enjoyable.

With James it was all so unfamiliar and therefore less relaxing. Even after six weeks they still weren't entirely comfortable during intimacy.

Movies portrayed first-time sex as easy and oh-so enjoyable. But real life was never like that. New partners were awkward with each other with neither knowing what the other expected or wanted. So although part of their sex life had settled into a type of normalcy, there was still that air of uncertainty lingering.

Even when he made small gestures like running his hand up her thigh, it felt so different to when Daniel did it. And when she looked down and saw a different hand on her leg, that too somehow seemed wrong.

Perhaps the problem was that she had moved on too quickly from one lover to another, because, somehow when she was in bed with James, she was still wishing it was Daniel with her instead.

The way the two men made love to her was very different. James was slower and more romantic. Daniel had been an eager lover which was something she preferred.

She had tried being more eager for James' body, but he always slowed things down to his own pace. It was still intense and exciting, but not her true preference.

Perhaps she just needed time to get over Daniel so that she could forget about how things used to be and just enjoy things as they were now, instead of always subconsciously comparing the two.

There was another problem that was plaguing her too. And that was how often she saw James. She knew that if he had his way, he'd be at her house every night and all weekend.

Lola enjoyed having time on her own, so she kept putting him off and making up excuses as to why she couldn't always be with him.

They spent most of their time at her house rather than his because he rented a room in a shared house. He said he did it because it was cheap and allowed him to save up to buy his own house faster.

James had been married once and it seemed as though his ex-wife had kept all of their assets, which didn't seem to bother him at all. He was so easy going that he'd simply moved out and moved on.

And now he wanted to spend all his spare time with Lola, but she didn't like that. It was hardest getting him to leave at the weekends.

He'd stay with her on Friday nights and then just hang around on Saturday. Even if she said she had to go out, he'd want to go with her so she'd have to be adamant that he couldn't come and had to leave.

The problem would then repeat itself on Sundays. He'd just hang around and not want to leave. Even if she went outside to tend her vegetable garden, he'd simply stay inside and put the TV on. He acted as though he lived there which annoyed her all the time.

Eventually she'd say 'Don't you need to go home?' or 'Don't you have things to do?' And after a while he'd take the hint and go.

Now it was Saturday again. They'd gotten up and she'd made coffee but not breakfast. Usually she'd make breakfast when he was there but this time she didn't. She wanted him to leave and thought that maybe he'd go sooner if he was hungry.

It wasn't because she didn't want to be with him. On the contrary, she was always happy to see him on Friday nights. But she needed him to know when he had out-stayed his welcome. And when he was still at her house even though they had no plans to be together all day, then he needed to go.

'No breakfast this morning?' he asked as they finished their coffee.

'I'm not hungry,' she lied.

'I am.'

'I'm not your cook.'

'Want me to make something?'

'Not here, no.'

'Lola is something wrong?'

They were sitting at the table on the back patio, looking out over the garden.

She put down her cup and turned to look at him. 'James, as much as I love being with you, I need to be on my own sometimes. I don't always want a guest for breakfast that I have to cook for. And I have things I need to do during the day so I need to get on and get going. And even on days when I don't have anything to do, I still want to be alone so that I can relax. I guess I'm just a bit of a loner deep down who needs her own space.'

He stared at her, his mouth slightly agape. 'You saying that you want to sleep with me at night but you don't want me around during the day?'

'No. Not at all. I do like seeing you during the day. If we have plans. But when we don't have plans then it's difficult for me if I always have a houseguest. Do you see what I mean?

'On the few occasions I stayed at your place, I had coffee and left the next morning and if we were seeing each other later, then I'd meet up with you again. But I never just stayed all day.'

'I thought that was because you didn't like being around my house mates.'

'No. It was because you're a single guy and I was giving you your space.'

James drained his cup and put it on the table. 'It's because we live apart, isn't it?'

'What is?'

'This problem. I've noticed it too. During the week you're busy working so we have to meet in the city for a quick drink when you've finished instead of me coming round here for the night.'

Lola said nothing. She couldn't tell him the truth that most of those days she hadn't even been at work and had only met him for a drink to put him off coming to her place. She didn't like him staying during the week when he had to get up early for work.

James continued. 'But if we lived together it wouldn't be a problem. We'd both be at home so we could do our own thing without having to trek out to meet each other for a quick drink, or me having to come round here all the time or you having to come to my place.'

Lola was stunned into silence. Eventually she said, 'Do you mean you want to live here? In my house?'

'Why not? It would be so much better.'

'For who?'

'For us both.'

'But I don't have a problem with us living apart, and we've only known each other for a few weeks.'

'Time doesn't matter. Just think. I'd bring my stuff here and we can be together all the time so that when we get up in the mornings you can do whatever you want because you won't have a house guest anymore.'

Oh God. He really wasn't getting it.

'James, I live alone because I like it this way.'

'So you never plan to live with someone?'

'This isn't a plan. You've just asked me if you can move your stuff in here so that you don't have to keep going home all the time. It's not a plan. It's just a convenience for you.'

'No it's not. I'm asking you to live with me.'

'No you aren't.'

'Yes I am.'

'OK. Then answer me this. Why do you want to live with me?'

'What do you mean?'

'See? The correct answer would be because you love me and want to build a life with me.'

'I do want to do that.'

'James. Don't insult me. We met less than two months ago and now you want to come and live in my house. We've never discussed our feelings for each other. Never.'

'Well of course I have feelings for you. I don't have to say it, do I?'

'James, this is pointless.'

'What is?'

'This whole conversation. I like you. I love being with you. But I don't want to live with you.'

'Will you ever want to?'

'How should I know? I have no idea how I'll feel about anything in a few months or years from now.'

'Months or years? It will take you that long to decide?'

'Why the sudden rush to live together?'

'It's not sudden. I've been thinking about it for a long time.'

'A long time? We've only known each other for six weeks.'

'Why are you so obsessed with time?'

'Why are you trying to get me to agree to something I don't want to do?'

'Living together is the next step in a relationship. It's how couples move on. If this relationship isn't moving on then there's no point in keeping it going.'

'Moving on? We've only just met! We're only just getting to know one another.'

'I thought we were closer than that.'

Lola stayed silent. There was nothing more to say. James wanted to move in and she didn't want him to.

He stood up. 'So this is it? You don't want to be with me?'

'Not permanently. But I like things as they are.'

He turned and left.

Lola sat there for a few minutes staring out into the garden. Although she was sorry to see James go, she wouldn't miss the intrusiveness of him always out-staying his welcome.

She thought they were just getting to know each other and enjoying being together. He thought he was moving in. And apparently he'd thought that all along.

How had she not noticed?

She sighed, stood up, picked up the cups and went inside to wash them.

Once the dishes were done she went into the bedroom, stripped the sheets from the bed and put them in the washing machine.

Without consciously thinking about it, she was washing James out of her life.

Chapter 14

Because James had left on Saturday morning, Lola now had no plans for the weekend.

She spent the morning catching up on some housework she'd been avoiding. After lunch she mowed the lawn. It didn't really need doing but she needed to be busy.

Then she showered and changed and walked into the city. She had absolutely no idea where she was going to go, but she just needed to keep moving. She ended up doing a circular walk.

She walked over the bridge to the south bank, passed by the Performing Arts Centre, along the full length of the walkways, and over the pedestrian bridge to the botanical gardens back on the north bank.

The gardens were a pleasant place to stroll and she walked along the path next to the river.

The path led to the main gate of the gardens and then to the Riverside walkway with its long row of cafés and restaurants all facing the river and Kangaroo Point on the other side. The view here was beautiful and it was further enhanced by the glorious weather.

She wandered into one of the bars and ordered a schooner of beer. There were plenty of tables outside so she chose one near the edge, away from other people, and sat down to watch the world go by. She was soon lost in her own thoughts as she sipped her drink and watched the boats on the river.

She'd often thought about buying an apartment in the city, one that overlooked the river and had a pool. But she enjoyed having her vegetable garden too much and knew that a few plant pots on a balcony just wouldn't be enough.

Maybe if she was rich and had a roof top apartment with a garden it might be different. But then again, no. It just wouldn't be the same as walking out into a proper garden.

But her choice of dwelling wasn't what she wanted to think about. She wanted to think about how she was feeling.

James had left her this morning. She told him she wasn't looking to move their relationship forward and he left.

Why was it that men always wanted to live with her? Why couldn't they live on their own? Women just seemed much more independent when they were single. Men, on the other hand, needed a mother replacement. She'd dated several men before she met Daniel and all of them eventually wanted to move in with her too.

That was what had been so easy about being with Daniel. He didn't want to live with her.

The problem, though, was that he was married, and although he didn't have an intimate relationship with his wife, he wouldn't leave her because she "needed" him which meant that Lola had to forever stay his dirty secret and could never be seen out in public with him.

She'd tried dating others, Rory and James, but it just wasn't the same. James' kiss and his touch didn't thrill her the way it did when Daniel touched her.

Of course, that could have been because she wasn't all that crazy about either of her new dates. Rory had disgusted her on their first and only date. And while James was really nice and she really liked him, the thrill just wasn't there.

With Daniel it had been different and even after two years she still thrilled at his touch. Just sitting here now thinking about it made her yearn. But the physical part of their relationship wasn't enough. She wanted a normal relationship with him and not to be hidden away as though she was something he was ashamed of.

She lifted her glass and drank the last mouthful of her beer. Looking at her watch she realised she'd been sitting there for about forty-five minutes. It hadn't felt that long at all. Man, she must have been deep in thought.

'Lola.' The voice made her jump even though it was familiar.

'George. Oh hi Angus. Great to see you both.'

'Are you waiting for someone?' asked George.

'No. Just sitting here trying to sort out a few emotional issues.' God! Why did she say that? She never discussed her personal life with her assistants.

'Good,' said George, clapping his hands together and smiling. Then he immediately changed his expression to something more somber and said, 'I mean, terrible that you've got emotional issues, but good because I can help you. I'm great with this sort of thing, aren't I Angus.'

'Yep,' he said slowly. 'You're certainly good with emotional issues. Other people's, of course,' he added.

George looked at him and grinned. 'Now. Now.' Then he looked back at Lola. 'How about if we all have a drink together and you can tell me what's troubling you?' Without waiting for an answer he pointed at her empty glass. 'What are you having?'

'A schooner of beer please. Heavy.'

To Angus George said, 'A schooner of heavy and I'll have my usual.'

Angus rolled his eyes to heaven and headed inside to the bar.

George sat down opposite her. 'So what's the issue? Is it something to do with your gentleman friend who used to turn up at the shop at the end of the day sometimes? I haven't seen him for a few weeks now and we have noticed how much work you started doing once he disappeared.'

He nodded knowingly as if he was divulging a well-hidden secret. 'You even went all out and remodeled the whole place. It actually provided Angus and I with a well-needed break when the shop was closed. We took advantage of the unexpected paid leave and spent a week at the coast.'

'That sounds wonderful. I wish I could have done the same.'

'But you couldn't because lover boy wasn't around. Am I right? You're a cagey one about him, you are. He keeps turning up but you never mention him and then he disappears and you throw yourself into your work without a word.

'Then we hear from Lindsay that the two of you went for a night out together and met two young men. So I thought lover boy must be out of the picture for good. So how is this new love of your life?'

Angus arrived carrying a small try with three drinks on it. He handed Lola her beer, put another in front of himself and a clear drink with ice in a tall glass in front of George.

He placed the tray on the end of the table, put her empty glass on it and sat next to Lola.

'Angus, I've just been bringing Lola up to speed on our observations about her love life.'

'You mean *your* observations,' said Angus without a smile. He always seemed so serious. Lola wondered if he ever relaxed and laughed.

'Oh come one,' said George affectionately. 'We've both been wondering what's going on.'

Angus didn't respond so Lola did. 'There isn't much to tell. Yes I did split up with the guy who used to meet me at the shop. We'd been dating for over two years and I did go out and meet someone else.'

'Are you still seeing him?' George cut in.

'Not as of today.'

'Oh my God. You must be broken hearted.'

'No. That's the thing. He was a really nice guy but something was missing from our relationship. It just wasn't magic. Do you know what I mean?'

George smiled. 'You mean it wasn't the same as it was with your previous lover? Not as good?'

Lola thought for a few seconds, not sure how to put how she felt into words. 'It was like that a bit. But at the same time I don't think it would have lasted anyway. I think comparing them just compounded the problem.'

George leaned forward and patted her hand. 'Oh dear. The answer is obvious but you just don't see it.'

'See what?'

'You're still not over your first love. I take it that you split over reasons other than you'd gone off him.'

'Yeah. We did.'

'And even though you don't want to be with him, you do.'

Lola smiled briefly. George was right. She wanted to not want to be with Daniel, but she did want to be with him.

In a soft voice George said, 'Sweetheart, the heart wants what the heart wants. Logic doesn't come into it. You can leave someone for what your head tells you are the right reasons, but your heart won't listen.'

'George, you're a psychic.'

'I know.'

'I want you to be wrong but you're right. I've been sitting here thinking of all the reasons why I shouldn't be with him. I've even tried to think of all the things about him that I hate that should make me glad to be away from him. But it still doesn't work.'

'Let me ask you this,' said George, holding her hand. 'Is he a bad person that you need to stay away from?'

'No. Quite the opposite. Sometimes I thought he was too nice for his own good, if you know what I mean.'

'Then why did you leave him if he's a great guy and you want to be with him?' This was from Angus.

It was such a simple question. He made it sound like an easy, cut and dried decision.

'It's a bit complicated.'

Angus responded again. 'No. You're trying to make it complicated. You're trying to give yourself reasons for not being with him but it's not working and all it's doing is causing you anguish and heartache.'

She knew that was it. That was exactly what was bothering her. Despite the problems of being with Daniel, it was far better to be with him and all his complications than be without him.

'He's right, isn't he?' said George.

'Yes, he is.'

'The question though is, what are you going to do about it?'

'That's easy. I'll see if he still feels the same.'

'I just hope for your sake he does and that he hasn't moved on and found someone new.'

'I doubt it. This isn't the first time we've split up, but it is the longest. He never looked for anyone else before.'

'Well no one's relationship is a bed of roses all the time. Even we've had our ups and downs, haven't we Angus?'

'*Must* we recount and dwell on those times?' Angus didn't smile as he spoke but Lola had the feeling that it wasn't because he was serious, but because he had a very dry sense of humor.

George laughed. 'Oh come on Angus. We got through it all didn't we?' And with that George began to regale them with one funny story after another about the ups and downs of their relationship.

Their one drink together turn into three and an order of chips, salad and garlic bread for all of them.

The next morning, Lola's head felt slightly sore, a result of having four drinks the night before.

It had been a great evening. George and Angus were great company and they had laughed a lot as George told stories and Angus feigned annoyance.

She'd caught a cab home rather than walk in the dark after she'd been drinking. Her limit was usually three drinks in a row otherwise she woke up with a hangover the next day. But she'd been having such a pleasant time that she wanted it to go on, so she'd had one more drink with them than she should.

They wanted to have another but Lola was at her limit if she wanted to stay sober, having already had a drink before George and Angus arrived.

She went home while they walked further on to find somewhere else to have another drink.

As she sat outside with her first coffee of the day, she thought over the advice they'd given her and knew what she had to do.

Chapter 15

Lola spent all week thinking about contacting Daniel. The only way she could get in touch was to call his office.

On Friday morning she made the call, not even knowing exactly what she would say to him.

He picked up on the second ring. She heard the familiar sound of his brisk, business-like greeting. It felt so wonderful to hear his voice.

'Hi. It's me. I wondered if we could meet.'

'Certainly,' he said, trying to pretend he was taking a business call.

'How about at my place after work.'

'Yes. I'm sure I can arrange that.'

'OK. See you soon.'

'Thanks. Bye.'

Lola felt relieved. He'd been so quick to agree to meet up with her again. She had wondered if he'd want to. She thought perhaps he might have decided to stay loyal to his wife or decided to find a different, less demanding, lover. God forbid.

Maybe he wanted to see her to say goodbye for good. She hoped not. All she knew right now was that she was going to see him again. She had butterflies in her stomach just thinking about it.

At 2.30p.m. her doorbell rang. She opened the door and let him in, and followed him into the living room. He turned to look at her, his expression neutral.

'I've missed you,' was all she said. Daniel took a step forward, wrapped his arms around her and kissed her passionately.

She felt the tension leave her body and her shoulders dropped. She hadn't even realised that she was tense. Being back in his arms was wonderful. She felt his erection as his body pressed tightly against hers. She orgasmed.

His touch and his kiss thrilled her like they always did. She loved the smell of him too.

She ran her hands down his back and over his buttocks. He moaned and kissed her harder, his tongue probing her mouth.

His hands moved up her body and over her breasts. She leaned back her head and moaned quietly.

His lips sought the soft flesh of her neck and he gently sucked and mouthed her skin.

His hands dropped to her hips. He grabbed the bottom of her T-shirt and lifted it up over her head and dropped it on the floor.

He put his face to her breasts and began kissing the skin between them.

She put her hands on the front of his shirt and began to unbutton it. Once the shirt was open she pushed it off his shoulders and it dropped to the floor. She leaned forward and began to kiss and stroke his bare chest.

He put his hands behind her and unhooked her bra. She wiggled and it fell to the floor in between them. She flicked it behind her with one foot.

Almost in unison they unzipped each other's pants and dropped them to the floor.

Lola stepped out of hers, but Daniel looked down at his feet and then up at her with a comical smirk. 'Oops. Shoes and socks problem.' Then it was her turn to laugh.

He bent down, untied his shoes and removed them one at a time and then his socks.

In the meantime, Lola removed her underpants. Daniel removed his trousers and underwear.

They stood naked for a brief moment, looking at each other.

Then she stepped forward. Daniel bent his head and mouthed her breasts and nipples. She ran her hands all over his body, down over this thighs and then up to his scrotum where she cupped her hand and squeezed gently.

He stopped what he was doing and groaned in pleasure.

She kissed his shoulder, her hands moving down his sides. Then she kissed his chest, his stomach, his abdomen, working her way down to his penis, which she took in her mouth as her hands fondled his buttocks.

By now they were both at the height of excitement. He touched and stroked her breasts as she knelt in front of him.

She was now so aroused, she was orgasming constantly.

When they finished foreplay he laid her down and he entered her. She was so excited she almost screamed.

His thrusting was hard and needy and as he finished, he shuddered repeatedly, thrusting hard again and again each time.

Afterwards, they were both completely spent. They lay on the living room rug beside each other, neither saying a word, and both breathing deeply.

Eventually Daniel spoke first. 'I missed you.'

'I could tell.'

'Really? How?' They both laughed.

It felt so good to be with him again, even to share his silly jokes.

Yet, she couldn't help but feel that something was different.

He put his arm around her and she snuggled up close to him. It felt so right to be together, yet changed.

Perhaps it was because she'd been sleeping with someone else, but she didn't think so. What she did with someone else shouldn't make any difference to the way she felt about Daniel.

She's read a book once about a woman who was crazy about a guy. They are together for years and constantly broke up and got back together again. They split up because he was unfaithful, yet she always still loved him, even though she didn't want to.

But after each breakup, there always seemed to be something different about the way she felt about him, as though a piece of her love for him was gone. Eventually she knew all the love would be gone and then she'd be able to leave him for good.

Is that what was happening now? Had Daniel's leaving her made her love him a little less?

It was hard to say for sure, but one thing she knew for certain was that it felt great to be back with him, she couldn't be happier, even though a little piece of her original happiness seemed to be missing.

But it didn't matter. All she wanted right now was to be with him again.

'Maybe we should get dressed?' His voice made her jump. She hadn't realised how deep in thought she was.

'Yeah, I guess.'

He turned and kissed her face, then sat up and looked around for his clothes.

Once they were dressed again she opened a bottle of wine and they sat out on the back patio.

'So,' he said. 'What's been happening lately?'

'With what?'

'With you.'

'Not much.'

'Must be something. I went past the shop one day and it was closed and there were workmen in there.'

'Just a part of the remodeling. And why were you at the shop? Were you looking for me or just checking up on me?'

'Neither. Just going somewhere and happened to walk past. Anyway, it would be hard to catch you at work because most days you're hardly there.'

'I've been there quite a bit recently with all the work that was going on. Especially afterwards because we had to restock the shelves and do all the cleaning up.'

He asked about the changes she'd made and she explained it to him.

Then he asked, 'And what else have you been up to?'

'How about you go first and tell me what you've been up to?'

He smiled at her and nodded. 'Oh, touché.'

'Well you made it abundantly clear that I can't ask you anything about your life, so right back at cha.'

'OK. Fair enough. Let's talk about us then. Is everything alright now?'

'Yeah, it is.'

'Can we carry on as normal then? I've really missed you.' He put his hand over the top of hers and gently squeezed it.

'I missed you too.' She meant what she said. She had missed him. But at the same time she also knew that things would never be the same again because something just felt different.

Chapter 16

Lola was now always aware of the something that felt different in their relationship. As the days and weeks rolled by she realised that what was different was that she felt less needy to be with him.

While she still wanted to see him, the change was that she didn't think about him all the time when they weren't together. This was great because it made her feel stronger and a lot less dependent on him.

It also changed the way she acted around him. She hadn't noticed it before but she previously had a tendency to touch him all the time and always wanted to snuggle up close. But now, although she still loved to do that, she didn't *need* to any more, and she did it less.

She also came to the realisation that, before their breakup, instead of wanting to have sex with him, she had been grateful, and that was a terrible way to feel, whether she was conscious of it or not.

And, because things had changed, she could now see clearly what was wrong with the way things were.

Lola had always been independently minded and liked living alone and running her own business.

Daniel was handy to have around because he wasn't there all the time and she knew he'd never want to live with her.

She was happy with the way things were. In fact, she was even happier now because she was less needy for his attention.

There was just one thing that still bothered her. They only saw each other when he had time to see her. She had never actually told him at any time that she wanted to see him on a day he wasn't there. It was just understood that he would see her when he had time.

They had a regular meeting on Friday afternoons when he finished work early and then on either Saturday or Sunday for dinner. It was never planned. It had always just happened that way. The rest of the week she didn't see him unless he could manage to get away and even then it was only for an hour or two for a drink and quick sex.

But it wasn't all bad. The time they spent together was great. She had no complaints about that. It was just the "only when he had time" thing which meant that she always had to be freely available.

She was laid in bed while she was thinking about it all. It was 9 a.m. on a Friday morning and she was enjoying the luxury of still being in bed while her staff were busy earning money for her.

Friday was a day she always saw Daniel. She would go into the shop on a Friday afternoon and he would call in when he'd finished work. Usually it was around mid-afternoon but sometimes later if he had to work longer to finish something off. So she would just loiter in the shop until he arrived.

Well, today would be different. She would go into work as usual but she'd leave before he got there and go out for the evening. It was just another leap forward in being more independent.

Daniel, of course, wouldn't like it at all. But what could he do? Demand that she wait around for him every Friday afternoon?

She stretched and got out of bed, showered and put on her dressing gown. In the kitchen she switched on the coffee machine and made toast.

She took her coffee and toast into the living room, switched on the TV and sat on the sofa with her legs outstretched and her back against a comfy cushion on the sofa's arm.

She picked up the remote control and channel-hopped until she found something worth watching. It was a one-hour crime show and it had just started. She watched it all the way through while she had her breakfast and a second cup of coffee from the machine.

When it was over, she washed the dishes, and then went upstairs to get dressed.

She put on a red cotton dress that was sleeveless, had a deep V-neckline, was shaped at the waist and went down to her mid-calf.

She brushed her hair and clipped it back at each side with flowery hair clips. It looked good.

When she arrived at the shop George wolf whistled. 'Good afternoon. And where are you off to today?'

'I'm going out to dinner and then for a few drinks.'

'Not seeing Mr. Wonderful tonight?'

'For a change, no.'

'Well they say it's as good as a rest.'

She put her handbag on a shelf behind the counter. 'How's it been today?' She looked around. There were quite a few people browsing around.

'Really busy. This morning we were rushed of our feet. Susan was here, of course, but she's gone now and thankfully it quieted down before she went.'

She saw Angus in one corner talking to a woman about their large Buddha Statue. They'd had it in stock for months which wasn't surprising because it was life-size and cost nearly a thousand dollars. But it was a beautiful ornament of the Buddha sitting cross-legged and holding a lotus flower in his hands.

George said, 'That woman was in here earlier looking at that and now she's back and has been talking with Angus for a while. I can't help but wonder how much there is to say about one item, no matter how big it is.'

'They're probably chatting about all things Buddhist.'

'Yeah, knowing Angus.'

'Is there any coffee out back?'

'No. There was until about half an hour ago but the pot's empty now.'

'I'll make some more.'

She disappeared into the back room, cleaned out the coffee machine and refilled it. As the coffee dripped through into the pot, she thought about where she was going to go. The markets were up on the south bank so she'd head over there first and have a stroll.

When there was enough coffee in the pot she poured herself a cup, returned the pot to its hotplate so it could carry on filtering and dripping, and went back out onto the shop floor.

The woman was now at the counter with Angus and handing him her credit card.

He looked up at Lola. 'Oh hi. Didn't see you come in. This lady has just bought our biggest Buddha. She'll come back tomorrow with her husband to pick it up.'

Lola smiled at the woman. 'Congratulations. It's a beautiful piece.'

'I know, and I have the perfect place for it. I can't wait to get it home.'

Lola looked at the large Buddha statue and wondered what they would fill the space with once it was gone.

She also thought that selling it after all these months was an auspicious sign that today was a lucky day. A good day to implement a new plan.

But she had no idea she was wrong.

She left the shop just before 2.30. George and Angus told her to have a great time but didn't ask where she was going or who with because they knew better. Lola never discussed her private life at work. In fact, she never discussed it with anyone.

While most women were natural chatterboxes, Lola had never been like that and preferred to only speak if there was something to say. She hated small talk and despised gossip.

So now she was off for a walk through the city, over the bridge and along the south bank to the markets.

Once over the bridge she stopped twice to watch some street performers and threw a couple of dollars into their collection tins.

By the time she reached the markets it was 4 o'clock and some of them had already started packing up, although most hadn't.

She browsed through the stalls, stopping to look briefly at a few things, with no intention of buying anything. She never saw the point in buying things she didn't need and most of these stalls were selling trinkets aimed at tourists.

She did, however, buy a hot cob of corn on a stick from a vendor selling just that and nothing else and doing what looked like a roaring trade.

The corncob was steaming so she walked back to the water park and sat on a bench to watch the kids playing while she ate. It was a gloriously hot day, just perfect for kids to spend time in the water.

She sat there for a while thinking that by now Daniel would have arrived at the shop to be told that she'd left and gone out for the evening. She wondered what he was thinking. Was he angry? Confused? Upset? Or all three?

She deposited the remains of her cob in a nearby bin and walked to the river and sat on a bench facing the water and watched the city on the north bank change from day to night.

Then she went to her favourite restaurant for dinner and sat quietly, watching the world around her as she ate salad and chips and drank a couple of cold beers.

When she was finished she slowly made her way back over to the city and then home.

By the time she got there she was exhausted and went straight to bed.

Chapter 17

They were stood in her kitchen, one either side of the breakfast bar.

Daniel was angry. She'd never seen him like this before.

'Lola, all I want to know is what the hell is going on?'

'I've told you. Nothing.'

'I came to the shop as usual yesterday only to find that you're not there. You're out on the town with God knows who doing goodness knows what.'

'That's it? Your jealous?'

'No! I just want to know why you left?'

'I wanted to have a night out but I knew you wouldn't take me. So what was I supposed to do?'

'You could have at least called me.'

'Why?'

'You knew I'd be coming to see you.'

'I'm not your property. I can do what I want. If you'd said you wanted to see me that would have been different. But you never do. You just turn up and expect me to be waiting every time.'

'But you *know* I always see you on Fridays. I always have.'

'Yeah, well, things are different now so don't *expect* anything. You forget that I'm single so I'm allowed to go out if I want.'

'You're in a relationship.'

'Not a committed relationship. You're not mine exclusively so you can't expect me to sit around and wait while you sit at home with another woman.'

'Oh, we're back to this old argument again are we?'

'We are if you keep making up rules about what I can and can't do. Never have I ever said that I will sit around every night and wait for you. But I do. And the one time I don't, this is how you react. You come here shouting at me and demanding answers. Well I can't ask *you* about things so you can't ask *me*!'

'What has gotten into you lately?' His voice was calmer. 'Ever since we got back together I feel as though something's changed. It's like you're trying to keep me at a distance all the time.'

'Yeah, well, maybe it's once bitten twice shy, as they say. When you walked out on me it hurt me so much and I was angry for making myself so vulnerable that you could hurt me so much.'

'I had no idea.'

'Either did I till it happened. But I promised myself that I wasn't going to let it happen again.'

'You mean you stopped caring about me as much?'

'I mean that I feel different now. Less needy. Less vulnerable. It's like, even though you've come back, it's no longer complete. Something is missing. Our relationship has changed. You must feel it too.'

He was thoughtful for a few seconds before he answered. 'Only because you're acting differently.'

'Yeah, well, it's just that some things will always stay between us and always bother me. Like your obsession with staying with your wife and that she "needs" you but you won't say why.' She made air quotes with her fingers when she said "needs."

His face flushed red. 'Let's not go there again.'

'OK. Let's get back to the present. You can't tell me what to do. And unless we have plans to meet, I can damn well do whatever I want and whatever I do is not your business.'

Daniel stared at her. 'It's as though you've suddenly become mean.'

'No. I've just woken up to this one-sided relationship.'

'I can't make definite plans to see you.'

'Why?'

'Because I can't. You just have to accept that.'

'What? Do you mean you can't because you're precious wife might suddenly "need" you?' She made air quotes again.

He stared at her but said nothing.

'Well it's about time things changed. You have to accept that I can't just sit around and wait for you all the time and if the opportunity arises for me to go out and have fun then I'll take it if I want to. I can't go out with you, can I?'

Daniel sounded weary when he spoke. 'Lola, this is exhausting. I can't do it anymore.'

He turned and walked away.

'See?' she yelled. 'This is why things were different this time. You always leave me.'

He didn't look back and within seconds he was gone.

Lola stood there for a few more minutes staring out the window.

He'd done it again. Walked out on her. She was furious, but she was also hurt.

She burst into tears and cried hard. Then she grabbed a couple of tissues from the tissue box near her, wiped her eyes, blew her nose, and threw the tissues in the bin. Then she opened a bottle of white wine, poured herself a glass and went into the living room to watch TV.

She wanted to relax and enjoy the evening. Tomorrow she would think about Daniel and decide what to do.

Chapter 18

The next morning Lola awoke with a mixed feeling of relief and apprehension. Relieved that she'd told Daniel how she felt. Apprehension about a possible future without him.

How many times could they argue over the same thing? She always wanted to ignore the fact that he was married and that they needed to hide whenever they were together. But no matter how many times she told herself it wasn't a problem, it was.

She got out of bed, washed, dressed and went downstairs to prepare breakfast.

She watched the morning news on TV while she ate and then wandered outside with her coffee.

She sat at the patio table and stared out across the back yard.

Whenever she was not with Daniel she was convinced that his need to hide her to protect his wife didn't matter. But when she was with him, it did matter. It irked her more and more as time went by.

She never understood his need to protect his wife's feelings, yet he was having an affair. And if he and his wife never had sex, then why did he stay with her? Their marriage couldn't be good if she never wanted to touch him. Or was it that he never wanted to touch her? Either way, it didn't make sense.

Then another thought struck her about his wife, one that she'd never thought of before. What if she didn't even exist? What if he was lying and he didn't have a wife at all?

That would explain his reluctance to talk about her.

No. She didn't think Daniel was a liar. Or even if he was, he couldn't be *that* devious. Could he?

She shook her head. She was being ridiculous.

And yet, there was something he wasn't telling her. He was always so adamant about them not being able to be seen out in public together AND that he would never talk about his wife or his life.

So many secrets. Too many secrets.

She went back into the kitchen and washed the few dishes she'd used.

Today was Sunday and the markets were on in the city along the riverbank.

She got ready and headed off to do some browsing. Just for a change, she decided to take the train. She hadn't done that in ages.

When she got to the station it was another fifteen minutes till the next train, so she sat on a bench and waited.

A few more people arrived as she sat there.

She thought again about Daniel and wondered if she'd ever see him again. One thing she did know was that each time he left her, she cared a little less about him when he returned, just like the woman in the book.

It was probably only a matter of time until they split up for good, which, if she was honest with herself, wasn't completely a bad thing if he was always going to choose his wife over her.

The trouble she had at the moment, was that while her head was telling her that it was time for a permanent break from him, in her heart she couldn't' do it. She still wanted to be with him. Just not on his terms any more. But that would never change. Just what the hell was it about his wife that made him so loyal to her and afraid of hurting her?

The train arrived and she boarded it along with everyone else. It wasn't too crowded and she managed to get a seat by herself.

It was only two stops before she had to get off. She stared out the window as the train began to move.

If...no, when, she corrected herself, she saw Daniel again she'd ask him once and for all about his wife. She'd insist that he tell her about his marriage and let him know how unhappy she was about him keeping secrets. Surely he cared just as much about hurting her as he did about hurting his wife?

Damn it! She deserved some answers after all this time.

Once off the train she made her way to the markets. It was another sunny day, typical of living here. Beautiful one day and perfect the next, as the saying goes, she thought to herself.

The markets were busy but not overly crowded. She moved from one stall to another, stopping to browse as she went.

She came across an organic fruit and vegetable stall and decided to buy some potatoes and carrots, the two things that she couldn't grow very easily in her back yard.

'Thanks,' she said as she was given her change. She turned away from the stall, change in one hand, purse in the other and shopping bag hanging off one arm, and saw that she was face to face with Daniel, and he was with a woman. By the surprised look on his face, it was obvious he hadn't recognised her until she'd turned around.

Lola didn't know what to do. She hoped her facial expression didn't look as shocked as she felt.

Daniel spoke quickly. 'Hi Lola.'

She looked directly into eyes, hoping to see some sort of signal of what she was supposed to say. 'Hey, Daniel.'

'Beautiful day for the markets, isn't it?' His voice seemed strange, a kind of fake happiness, and his smile was not as broad and friendly as usual.

She thought she'd better tread carefully and keep the conversation neutral. 'It certainly is. I wasn't expecting to see you here though.'

'Oh, well, you know. It's nice to be outdoors after begin cooped up in the office all week.' He looked guilty. She hoped she didn't too.

The woman continued to smile at her but Lola kept her eyes on Daniel and he stared straight back at her.

Without breaking their gaze he said, 'This is Lola, a colleague from work. Lola this is my wife, Claire.'

Bam! Just like that. The illusive wife. She really did exist.

Lola inhaled before she turned her gaze to the woman and smiled. 'Claire. So lovely to meet you.' The woman continued to smile at her but said nothing.

Lola's smile was frozen on her lips. She didn't know what else to say. She didn't want to say anything. She just wanted to get out of there.

If they were in a comedy show, she would have turned and run screaming in the opposite direction, dropping money and vegetables as she went.

But it wasn't a comedy show, and it wasn't funny. So instead she said, 'Well, as lovely as it is to see you both, I'm in a hurry and have to be somewhere soon. Goodbye Claire,' she said, smiling at his wife.

Then she looked Daniel firmly in the eye, her smile disappearing quickly. 'Goodbye Daniel.' She emphasized the word "goodbye" as she spoke.

'Bye,' he mumbled.

He looked hurt but she also knew that he understood.

She turned and walked briskly away without looking back, tears brimming as she went.

Daniel watched her until she disappeared into the crowds.

He looked at down Claire and sighed. Then he took out his handkerchief and wiped away the small amount of saliva coming from the corner of her mouth before adjusting her into a more upright position.

And as he grasped the handles of her wheelchair, he knew he'd never see Lola again.

End.